## What Kids Say About
## Carole Marsh Mysteries . . .

*"I love the real locations! Reading the book always makes me want to go and visit them all on our next family vacation. My Mom says maybe, but I can't wait!"*

*"One day, I want to be a real kid in one of Ms. Marsh's mystery books. I think it would be fun, and I think I am a real character anyway. I filled out the application and sent it in and am keeping my fingers crossed!"*

*"History was not my favorite subject till I starting reading Carole Marsh Mysteries. Ms. Marsh really brings history to life. Also, she leaves room for the scary and fun."*

*"I think Christina is so smart and brave. She is lucky to be in the mystery books because she gets to go to a lot of places. I always wonder just how much of the book is true and what is made up. Trying to figure that out is fun!"*

*"Grant is cool and funny! He makes me laugh a lot!!"*

*"I like that there are boys and girls in the story of different ages. Some mysteries I outgrow, but I can always find a favorite character to identify with in these books."*

*"They are scary, but not too scary. They are funny. I learn a lot. There is always food which makes me hungry. I feel like I am there."*

# What Parents and Teachers Say About Carole Marsh Mysteries . . .

*"I think kids love these books because they have such a wealth of detail. I know I learn a lot reading them! It's an engaging way to look at the history of any place or event. I always say I'm only going to read one chapter to the kids, but that never happens—it's always two or three, at least!"*
*—Librarian*

*"Reading the mystery and going on the field trip—Scavenger Hunt in hand—was the most fun our class ever had! It really brought the place and its history to life. They loved the real kids characters and all the humor. I loved seeing them learn that reading is an experience to enjoy!"*
*—4th grade teacher*

*"Carole Marsh is really on to something with these unique mysteries. They are so clever; kids want to read them all. The Teacher's Guides are chock full of activities, recipes, and additional fascinating information. My kids thought I was an expert on the subject—and with this tool, I felt like it!"*
*—3rd grade teacher*

*"My students loved writing their own Real Kids/Real Places mystery book! Ms. Marsh's reproducible guidelines are a real jewel. They learned about copyright and more & ended up with their own book they were so proud of!"*
*—Reading/Writing Teacher*

*"The kids seem very realistic—my children seemed to relate to the characters. Also, it is educational by expanding their knowledge about the famous _____ books."*

*They _____ _____ _____ and adventures with children _____ _____."*

*_____ _____ for pleasure."*

*_____ _____ _____ be used for reluctant readers, and _____*

*is*

# The Mystery at the

# Maya
# Ruins

## MEXICO

by Carole Marsh

Gallopade International is introducing SAT words that kids need to know in each new book we publish. The SAT words are bold in the story. Look for this special logo beside each word in the glossary. Happy Learning!

Gallopade is proud to be a member and supporter of these educational organizations and associations:

**American Booksellers Association**
**American Library Association**
**International Reading Association**
**National Association for Gifted Children**
**The National School Supply and Equipment Association**
**The National Council for the Social Studies**
**Museum Store Association**
**Association of Partners for Public Lands**
**Association of Booksellers for Children**
**Association for the Study of African American Life and History**
**National Alliance of Black School Educators**

# 30 Years Ago . . .

As a mother and an author, one of the fondest periods of my life was when I decided to write mystery books for children. At this time (1979), kids were pretty much glued to the TV, something parents and teachers complained about the way they do about web surfing and video games today.

I decided to set each mystery in a real place—a place kids could go and visit for themselves after reading the book. And I also used real children as characters. Usually a couple of my own children served as characters, and I had no trouble recruiting kids from the book's location to also be characters.

Also, I wanted all the kids—boys and girls of all ages—to participate in solving the mystery. And, I wanted kids to learn something as they read—something about the history of the location. And I wanted the stories to be funny. That formula of real+scary+smart+fun served me well.

I love getting letters from teachers and parents who say they read the book with their class or child, then visited the historic site and saw all the places in the mystery for themselves. What's so great about that? What's great is that you and your children have an experience that bonds you together forever—something you shared; something you all cared about at the time; and something that crossed all age levels: a good story, a good scare, and a good laugh!

30 years later,

*Carole Marsh*

Christina "Mystery Girl" Mimi Papa Grant

Hey, kids! As you see—here we are ready to embark on another of our exciting Carole Marsh Mystery adventures! You know, in "real life," I keep very close tabs on Christina, Grant, and their friends when we travel. However, in the mystery books, they always seem to slip away from Papa and me so that they can try to solve the mystery on their own!

I hope you will go to www.carolemarshmysteries.com and apply to be a character in a future mystery book! Well, the *Mystery Girl* is all tuned up and ready for "take-off!"

Gotta go...Papa says so! Wonder what I've forgotten this time?

Happy "Armchair Travel" Reading,

*Mimi*

# About the Characters

 **Christina:** Mysterious things really do happen to her! Hobbies: soccer, Girl Scouts, anything crafty, hanging out with Mimi, and going on new adventures.

 **Grant:** Always manages to fall off boats, back into cactuses, and find strange clues—even in real life! Hobbies: camping, baseball, computer games, math, and hanging out with Papa.

 **Mimi** is Carole Marsh, children's book author and creator of Carole Marsh Mysteries, Around the World in 80 Mysteries, Three Amigos Mysteries, Baby's First Mysteries, and many others.

 **Papa** is Bob Longmeyer, the author's real-life husband, who really does wear a tuxedo, cowboy boots and hat, fly an airplane, captain a boat, speak in a booming voice, and laugh a lot!

Travel around the world with Christina and Grant as they visit famous places in 80 countries, and experience the mysterious happenings that always seem to follow them!

# Books in This Series

# Table of Contents

**Mexico**

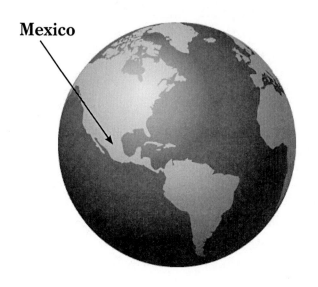

YUCATAN
PENINSULA

MEXICO

MAYA RUINS

# 1

# Shore Leave

"Mimi! Papa! Grant's missing!" yelled Christina, racing up to her grandparents. Her long brown hair flew behind her as she ran. Mimi and Papa stood on a street corner studying a map of Cozumel, Mexico. They were hard to miss—Mimi in her favorite red cowboy boots and jeans, and Papa sporting scuffed leather boots and a white Stetson hat.

"He was there one second...and then POOF!...he just disappeared!" Christina exclaimed in breathless bursts. "We were at that antique shop over there," she continued, pointing in the direction of a bright blue building. "The next thing I knew...Grant was gone!"

"Don't worry, Christina, we'll find him," said Papa, throwing his burly arm around her shoulders. "We always do," he added reassuringly.

"Well, we'd better find him quickly," warned Mimi. "Our cruise ship will be departing soon, and you know what the announcement said about no-shows."

"They get left behind!" cried Christina. Her mind raced. "What if Grant was kidnapped?" Grant could be a royal pest sometimes, but she shuddered at the thought of her little brother in the hands of kidnappers.

"Well, if that's the case, I pity the poor kidnappers," joked Papa. "I expect they will soon be paying us to take him back," he added with a grin.

"Be serious, Papa," Mimi said. "We have a missing grandchild on our hands in the middle of Cozumel, Mexico."

"Okay, then," said Papa, winking at Christina. "Let's try these side streets. One of us is bound to find him."

Just around the corner, Grant stood alone in an alley off the main street. He gazed at a spiky, gray iguana sunning itself on a vine-covered, white stucco wall. "Hey, buddy," said Grant. "Nice to meet you!"

The scaly iguana stared back at him with its beady gray eyes. It began bobbing its head up and down. Grant knew from his *Reptiles of Mexico* book that iguanas communicate this way, altering the number and frequency of bobs to mean different things.

Grant got down on his hands and knees to imitate his new-found friend. He bobbed his head up and down, too. The iguana flicked its tongue in and out of its mouth. Grant did the same. It moved its head from side to side. Grant followed suit. It slowly whisked its gray-and-brown-striped tail back and forth. Grant wagged his behind iguana-style.

"Hey, I can speak iguana!" exclaimed Grant. He had visions of himself starring in his own TV series—*The Iguana Whisperer*.

Just then, Christina and Mimi turned the corner onto the alley. Shocked speechless, the pair watched the spectacle before them. Grant was crawling around on the ground, bobbing his head, flicking his tongue, and wiggling his behind from side to side.

Christina nudged Mimi and whispered, "Do you think he has heatstroke or something?"

"Hmmm," Mimi replied, "maybe it's Montezuma's Revenge." She crossed her arms and peered over the top of her sparkly, red-rimmed sunglasses.

"Revenge?" wondered Christina. She thought her grandmother might be kidding. Being a mystery writer, Mimi often shared fascinating and sometimes weird facts with her grandchildren. "But, who would want revenge on Grant?" she asked.

Mimi smiled. "Don't worry," she said. "That's just another way of saying he has a bad tummy-ache."

"Oh," said Christina. Then she spied the iguana perched on the wall.

"Argggh!" cried Christina, stamping her foot. "Hey, lizard boy, snap out of it!" she yelled. "You're going to make us miss the ship!"

Jolted back to reality, Grant sprang to his feet. The startled iguana launched itself off the wall and landed smack on top of Grant's fuzzy, blonde head.

"Yaaaaah!" Grant screamed. "Get it off! It's going to eat my brain!" Grant spun around in circles, pawing the air around his head.

THUD! Grant landed, bottom first, in the dusty alleyway, sending the iguana flying through the air. It landed on a soft patch of grass and scampered off into the bushes.

"You have some serious explaining to do, young man," said Mimi. "But right now, we have to *vamanos*!"

"*Vama*-what?" asked Grant, dizzy from his iguana encounter.

"It means 'Let's go' in Spanish!" shouted Christina, as she pulled Grant up by his arm and led him toward the main street.

Spotting Papa, the trio ran to him.

"Mission accomplished, I see," boomed Papa. "Glad to see you're okay, kiddo."

"We're going to miss the ship!" wailed Christina. "This way!"

The group raced to the pier, arriving out of breath. They were too late! The massive ship had pulled away from the dock. A rolling wake rippled behind it.

"What are we going to do now?" exclaimed Christina. "All of our stuff is on board!"

*In the small space between two metal shipping crates just unloaded onto the docks crouched a man wearing a shiny white suit. He waited in the shadows, watching their every move and listening to their every word!*

## ••

# 2

# When in Rome...

"Unless we can swim super-fast, catch hold of a giant ship with our bare hands, and climb up the side, I'd say we were stranded!" exclaimed Grant.

"If you hadn't wandered off, we wouldn't be in this mess," shouted Christina.

"Well, if you hadn't dragged me over to that shop to look at boring old junk, I wouldn't have wandered off!" returned Grant.

Christina shot back, "Well, if you hadn't—"

"Quiet down," Papa commanded. "I'm on the phone with the cruise line now."

After a few minutes, Papa clicked off his phone. "The good news is they put our luggage in storage on the ship. The bad news is the ship doesn't return here for another five days."

"So, what are we supposed to do until then?" Christina whined. "All we have are the clothes on our backs!"

"Well," said Mimi with a twinkle in her eye, "'When in Rome...'" Her voice trailed off, as she began scrolling through her phone's contact list. She dialed a number.

"Wait, we're in Rome? As in Rome, Italy?" asked Grant. "Let's get some pizza!"

Christina sighed. "Grant, we're still in Mexico. 'When in Rome, do as the Romans do' is just an expression. It means you do as the locals do."

"Oh!" Grant replied. "So, does that mean no pizza?"

"Nope, no pizza," said Christina.

"Listen up, children," Mimi said above the din of the screeching seabirds. "A dear old college friend of mine lives just north of the Yucatan Peninsula. It's a short plane ride but we'll need to leave *pronto*! Papa, put that ten-gallon hat of yours to good use and hail us a taxi!"

In the taxi, Grant said, "I had a yucky tan once. Well, it was more like a really bad sunburn." He rubbed his neck as if remembering how much it hurt.

"No, Grant. It's not 'yucky tan'," said Christina. "It's you-kah-tahn! The Yucatan Peninsula is where we are now. We'll be flying to an island just north of the peninsula, right, Mimi?"

"That's right, Christina," Mimi answered. "My friend moved to the island after retiring."

After a weaving ride through mid-day traffic that left everyone a bit woozy, they rushed to the ticket counter at the small airport.

"I am so sorry," explained the clerk, a middle-aged man with gentle eyes, "but our pilot just took off."

"But, sir," said Mimi. "I just called you twenty minutes ago to book the plane!"

"The man who came here before you said the reservation was for him," the clerk explained.

"Is there nothing you can do?" Mimi asked.

"No, not unless you carry a valid international pilot's license for a small plane, *Señora*!" the man half-joked. "We have two planes, but only one pilot."

"Well, it just so happens..." said Papa, stepping forward and plopping his license down on the counter. "I never leave home without it!"

Soon, they were flying over white sailboats dotting the clear turquoise waters of the Caribbean Sea.

"Look, there's the island," announced Papa.

"It looks so mysterious," said Christina.

"Don't say 'mysterious'," groaned Grant. "It sounds too much like 'mystery'! And mystery means solving clues when I'd rather be eating!"

"Don't worry," said Mimi. "We're just going to relax for a few days—just until the ship returns to Cozumel. I'm sure there is no mischief waiting for us on such a small island."

"Famous last words," said Papa with a hearty laugh. He banked the plane down toward the small airstrip below. "Hang on, crew! We're in for a bumpy landing!"

# 3

# Welcome to Casa Iguana!

Papa helped Mimi and the kids down off the wing of the plane and onto the sunbaked runway.

"Carole, it's been ages!" exclaimed a trim, dark-haired woman.

"Esmeralda!" Mimi said as they hugged. "Thank you so much for meeting us here! Has it been ten years already?"

"At least," the woman replied.

"It was mighty kind of you to help us find a place on such short notice!" said Papa.

Esmeralda laughed. "So glad you could 'drop in'! It must be nice to have a pilot in the family!" She winked at Mimi.

She turned to the children. "You must be Christina and Grant. You will have to meet my grandchildren, Eva and Miguel. They are here on vacation, too. You know," she said with a smile, "your Mimi is a favorite of theirs! They have read all of her mysteries!"

"Everyone," Mimi said, "this is my dear friend, Professor Esmeralda Zapo."

"*Mucho gusto*, nice to meet you all," said the woman. "Please, call me Professor Z. That is what my students at the university used to call me."

"Professor Z was a marine biology professor at La Salle University in Cancun," explained Mimi.

"Yes, I'm retired now," Professor Z said, "but I couldn't quite give up my passion for ichthyology."

"Are you one of those doctors who puts people to sleep before an operation?" asked Grant.

"No, Grant!" said Christina. 'That's *anesthesiology*. Professor Z is an *ichthyologist*. She studies fish," explained Christina.

"That's right, Christina," Professor Z remarked. "I'm actually doing some fascinating work on whale sharks. But I'll tell you more about that tomorrow. I think you'll like the hotel—especially you, Grant. It has a *cool* name. At least that's what my grandchildren tell me."

"What's it called?" asked Grant excitedly.

"Casa Iguana," replied Professor Z. "That means House of the Iguana. And it's right on the beach!"

The color drained from Grant's face. Christina couldn't keep from giggling.

After a short ride on the golf-cart taxi, the gang arrived at Casa Iguana. Bright pink and red bougainvillea flowering vines spilled from giant flowerpots at the entrance to the hotel. The kids piled onto the comfortable sofas in the waiting area.

"Okay, you're all checked in. Christina, here is the key to your room—room 18,"

Professor Z said. "You're right across from your grandparents."

She gave Mimi the address to her home and promised to meet them the next day for breakfast.

Christina unlocked the door and placed the key on the bedside table. A small light was on. The air conditioner hummed softly.

"Grant, are you looking for iguanas under the bed?" asked Christina.

Grant was on his hands and knees, peeking under the bed. "I'm sure this place is called Casa Iguana for a reason!" he said.

"You've got iguanas on the brain," said Christina, kicking up her legs and landing perfectly in the middle of her bed.

She grabbed her backpack and dumped its contents next to her. She found her journal and opened it.

Plop! A jade stone fell into her lap. "Hey, what's this?" she exclaimed. She held the shiny green stone up to the light. It was jagged on two sides.

Grant popped up from the floor. "You found an iguana?" he asked, looking around wildly.

"No, I found this in my backpack." Christina said. "I bet it's jade!"

Carved on the front of the stone was the head of a strange-looking feathered snake.

Christina flipped the stone over. On the back were some unusual symbols.

"Can I see it?" asked Grant. He took it and held it up to the light. "Oh, this was in that shop you dragged me to."

"You saw this there? But, how do you remember this one stone? You weren't even in the shop for very long!" cried Christina.

"Look at it! It's cool! Snakes—feathers—shiny green stone! All the stuff I love!" Grant said. "I saw a guy pick it up and study it with a magnifying glass. Maybe *he* put it in your bag."

"What? Why would anyone do that?" Christina huffed and took the stone back from Grant.

"How would I know? He had it last," Grant wailed. "If you don't want it, I'll take it."

Christina quickly closed her hand before Grant could grab it back. "No way!" she said. "If it really came from that shop, then it doesn't belong to us! We'll have to return it as soon as we get back to Cozumel."

"I guess," pouted Grant.

"It's got to be mythological!" Christina said.

"What? Mytha-*what*-ical?" asked Grant, scrunching his brow.

"Mythological," Christina repeated.

Grant turned to look in the mirror. He repeated the word, stretching his cheeks down with his hands. "Mythological...mythological... mythological," he repeated softly. "What's mythological?"

"It's like folklore, legends, fables...you know, stories from a long time ago," Christina answered. "I noticed these strange symbols on the back," she said. "I wonder what they are."

"Oh, those are Maya symbols for numbers," said Grant.

"What makes you think that?" asked Christina.

"All the dots and lines," he said. "I found a book about the Maya numbering system on the plane over here."

"On the plane?" Christina asked. "And I thought you were just wasting your time fogging up the window to draw weird faces on it," she said.

"I'll prove it to you," Grant replied. "And anyway, those were Maya numbers, not faces!"

He wrote the equation on a piece of hotel stationery. "There!" he said, pointing to his math. "The dots are worth one and the lines are worth five. The bottom symbol is in the 1's place, and the top symbols are in the 20's place."

"You mean the 10's place, right?" asked Christina.

"No, the Maya had a 20's place," Grant explained. "The top number is 3 plus 5 plus 5 plus 5. That's 18. Since it's in the 20's place, you multiply it by 20."

"I see," said Christina. "The bottom is just 5, right?"

"Right!" said Grant.

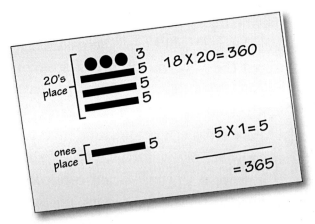

"Then, what do you do?" asked Christina.

"You just add the 360 from the 20's place and the 5 from the 1's place," explained Grant.

"365?" guessed Christina.

"Yep! Believe me now?" asked Grant.

"Yes! I'm impressed! I guess the iguana didn't eat all of your brain!" joked Christina.

Grant rubbed his head, remembering the iguana attack.

●●●●

# 4

# Isla Holbox

The next morning, Professor Z and her grandchildren met Mimi, Papa, Christina, and Grant sitting outside at the café.

"*Buenos dias*! Good morning!" said Professor Z. A boy and a girl around the same ages as Grant and Christina stood beside her.

"Good morning to you, too," said Mimi. Papa stood up to greet them.

"Christina and Grant," Professor Z said, "I'd like you to meet Eva and Miguel, my grandchildren. They are staying here on the island with me for the summer."

"Hello!" said Eva. She was about the same height as Christina, but she had jet-black hair and bright brown eyes. "After we finish eating, we'll show you around town. And we brought some clothes for you to wear while you're here. I hope you like them!"

"Thanks!" Christina said. "So, you heard we missed our cruise ship?"

Eva looked at Grant and giggled. "Yes, we heard."

"What's the name of this island, anyway?" asked Grant.

"Isla Holbox," said Miguel.

Eva explained, "Well, it's spelled H-O-L-B-O-X, but it's pronounced 'Holbosh.' The x makes a *sh* sound."

"Holbox means black hole!" said Miguel. Miguel was a whole foot shorter than his older sister, but he had the same jet-black hair and big brown eyes.

"Black hole?" Grant repeated. "Like the ones in outer space?"

"No," said Miguel, smiling. "Actually, the water on the south side of the island is kind of black. That's where the name comes from."

*Isla Holbox*

"Isn't *negro* the Spanish word for black?" asked Christina.

"Yes," said Eva, "but Holbox isn't a Spanish word. It's Mayan. Mayan is the language of the native people who lived in this area of Mexico before the Spanish colonized it."

"Do you speak Mayan?" asked Grant.

"Only a few words," said Miguel.

"Grant speaks another language," Christina announced. "It's called Iguanan." She stuck her tongue out at Grant and wagged her back end iguana-style.

"Aaah! I'll get you!" Grant shouted, jumping out of his chair and chasing after his laughing sister.

"Wait for us!" Eva and Miguel shouted, running after them.

The kids strolled along a sidewalk lined with brightly painted buildings. A light breeze took the edge off the summer heat.

"Your grandmother is an ichthyologist?" asked Christina.

"Yes, she is," Eva replied. "She's doing research on whale sharks."

"Is a whale shark a mix between a whale and a shark?" asked Grant.

Eva laughed. "Actually, whale sharks aren't whales at all," she said. "They're a type of shark, and sharks are a kind of fish. The whale part comes from their size."

"They're the largest fish in the world," Miguel added.

"Are they dangerous?" asked Christina.

"No, not at all," replied Eva. "They're very gentle. They eat mostly plankton. They come to the tip of the Yucatan every year around this same time. It's their favorite feeding ground."

"Well, I wouldn't get too close to their big mouth," warned Miguel. "You might get sucked in!"

"Hey," Eva said excitedly, "we're going out on the boat later on today, if the weather holds up. Grandmother's research team is planning to dive with the whale sharks, and we're going with them."

"You should come," Miguel suggested.

"Count me in!" said Christina.

"Me too!" said Grant. "We'll have a whale of a time!"

# 5

# Boat Bumps and Tattoos

The crystal clear water of the Caribbean Sea lapped at the boat, rocking it gently from side to side. Dark clouds were forming on the horizon. Christina noticed a small kayak not far from where they were anchored.

The man in the kayak wore a shiny, white suit and a fisherman's hat. He waved nervously, adjusted his hat, and quickly looked away.

BAM! BAM! The boat rocked wildly.

"Hang on, everyone!" shouted Papa. He caught Grant mid-air.

"Papa, we're being attacked! Iguanas can't swim, can they?" asked Grant.

"I guess we'll soon find out," answered Papa, still hanging on to Grant.

"It's coming for the boat again!" shouted one of the scientists.

"It can't be!" cried Professor Z. "It is! It's Oliver!"

Everyone scooted to the starboard side of the boat. An enormous whale shark with giant spots on its back scooted past their boat, bumping it gently.

"He's come to say hello!" cried Professor Z.

"You named him Oliver?" asked Christina.

"Yes! Oliver is the largest whale shark ever sighted in these waters," Professor Z explained.

"How big is he?" asked Grant.

"About 40 feet long, and he weighs more than 10 tons," she said. "We've wanted to put a tracking device on him for some time now."

Christina asked, "Why would you want to do that?"

"We want to track his movements, so we can monitor his migration patterns. It might help us protect him and other whale sharks like him," Professor Z explained.

"Grandmother, is someone trying to hurt Oliver?" asked Eva.

"Let's just say it's better to be safe than sorry," Professor Z replied. "Besides, they are fascinating creatures worth protecting. And, they're important to the ecosystem of this area."

"We're ready," announced Emilio, one of Professor Z's assistants.

The kids pulled on their diving masks and snorkels and slid off the side of the boat and into the water, following Emilio.

"Emilio will attach an electronic tracker to Oliver using this long pole," Professor Z shouted to them. "It has a special code, so only we can track him. Remember," she warned, as they bobbed on the surface of the clear blue water, "you can swim up to Oliver, but you can't touch him. Do you understand?" The kids all nodded in agreement.

"Follow me!" shouted Emilio, before disappearing below the surface.

The kids watched as the huge creature **meandered** along under them. Its massive gills flapped open and closed as it moved silently through the water.

Emilio motioned for the kids to dive a few feet deeper. Kicking their flippers as hard as they could, the gang caught up to Oliver's face. Peering back at the kids was a giant black eye.

Emilio easily attached the electronic tracker to Oliver's side. He motioned for the kids to go up. Slowly, Oliver turned and started out for deeper waters, swishing his tail goodbye.

The kids popped up to the surface. "Awesome!" they cried in unison. They high-fived each other excitedly.

One by one, Emilio pulled the kids out of the water and into the boat. Christina waited patiently for her turn to be pulled out.

*Boat Bumps and Tattoos*

Dark clouds billowed overhead. The wind picked up speed, making the water choppy and dark. The kayak that Christina had noticed before was being pushed closer to their vessel by the wind. A shiny, white suit jacket was draped over one side, but the man was gone!

Christina dove under the water's surface to see if the man had jumped in. She suddenly felt very protective of Oliver. A school of brightly colored fish scurried past her.

SPLASH!

"Grant!" sputtered Christina, as she made it to the surface. Grant had plunged back into the water.

"Sorry, Christina!" apologized Grant. "I slipped!"

*As Emilio reached out his hand to Christina, she spied a small red tattoo on the inside of his*

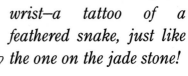

*wrist—a tattoo of a feathered snake, just like the one on the jade stone!*

# 6

# The Mysterious 365

The kids made it back to Casa Iguana seconds before the sky cracked with lightning. Grant munched on a mango in their room.

"I'm telling you, Grant, the two have to be connected!" Christina said.

"Nah! Just because some guy has a tattoo of a feathered snake on his wrist doesn't mean there's some big mystery to solve," he said between juicy bites.

"But the stone—it has that same exact symbol," Christina said.

   31

"I'll bet it's a common symbol in Mexico. There is something weird about Tattoo Guy, though," Grant said.

"Weirder than the snake tattoo? OK, tell me," Christina challenged.

"Well, today, on the boat, I didn't really slip," admitted Grant.

"You didn't slip? You mean you fell on me on purpose?" asked Christina.

"No! And it wasn't *on* you, it was *next to* you!" he said defensively. "Emilio was pulling me out, but then he let go, and I fell back in."

"Emilio let you fall in? Aha! Probably so I wouldn't see Kayak Man swimming around," Christina reasoned.

"Kayak Man? What kayak?! What man?!" demanded Grant.

Christina told her brother about the man in the white suit and fisherman's hat. "All of it— the jade stone, Emilio the Tattoo Guy, and now Kayak Man—they're connected for sure!"

Just then, a note slipped under the door. Grant hopped off the bed and picked it up. He showed it to Christina.

**365**

**91 in 4 directions, a ball
of fire warms its top!**

"Is this some type of clue? What do you think it means?" Christina said.

Grant wasn't listening. He was sprawled on the floor, peeking under the hotel door into the hallway.

"What are you doing? Looking for more iguanas?" Christina asked.

"No, I'm looking for shoes," said Grant. "If we know who left the clue, we can just ask them what it means. Saves time, right?"

"Oh, Grant!" said Christina. "Everyone's waiting for us at the café!"

Papa met the kids at the café entrance. "What an experience you all had this morning swimming with the whale sharks!" he exclaimed.

"It was so fun, Papa!" cried Grant between smoothie slurps. "Oliver was super gigantic!

He has a huge mouth that goes like this!" He demonstrated by pulling and stretching his face. Everyone, including the waiter, laughed at Grant's facial **contortions**.

"Professor Z, Eva mentioned that the Maya used to live in this area of Mexico," Christina said.

"Yes, they did," replied Professor Z, still giggling from the show Grant put on. "The Yucatan Peninsula was inhabited long ago by the Maya people. For many centuries, they ruled the area. In fact, they're still here!" she said.

"What do you mean?" asked Grant.

"Well, Grant, you're looking at a real live Maya right now!" she replied.

"Whoooooa!" said Grant. "You mean you're a real live Maya?"

"I certainly am," Professor Z said with a big smile.

"Does a feathered snake have anything to do with Maya culture?" asked Christina.

"Oh, does it ever!" Professor Z answered. "The feathered serpent was a religious symbol to the Maya. The feathers represented the ability to fly like a god and the serpent represented the ability to move among the people."

A shiver ran down Christina's spine at the mention of snakes moving among the people.

Professor Z continued, "The Maya built a huge pyramid dedicated to the feathered serpent god. You can see their pyramid at the Chichen Itza ruins on the mainland."

"And at night," Mimi said, "they put on a light show. Tomorrow is July 16, the start of the Maya New Year. So, if you kids are interested in a little sightseeing, tomorrow should be pretty special."

"Well, this sure sounds like an adventure in the making for you kids!" said Papa.

"Yessss!" exclaimed Grant. He high-fived Miguel in excitement.

"Great!" exclaimed Professor Z. "My niece Izzy has her own tour business. She graduated from my alma mater with a degree in archaeology, so she is quite the expert on Chichen Itza!"

# 7

# Itchy Chickens!

The next morning, Mimi and Papa joined the kids on the 30-minute *Nine Hermanos* ferry ride from the island of Holbox to Chiquila on the mainland. Professor Z's niece, Izzy, met them there.

"The 'Lime-O-Zeen' is here!" cried Grant.

"Ooh, I like that name!" said Izzy, as she helped the kids into her lime-green tour van. Izzy sported bug-eyed sunglasses and a floppy yellow hat.

As Izzy revved her engine, she announced, "Next stop: the ruins of Chichen Itza. Buckle up, sit back, and relax."

Through the window of the van, the kids waved good-bye to Mimi and Papa.

Grant poked his seatmate Miguel in the ribs as they bounced along in Izzy's van. "Hey, I've got a joke," Grant said over the clicking of the motor. "Why did the itchy chicken cross the road?"

"I don't know, why?" Miguel asked.

"So he could get to the back scratcher on the other side!" joked Grant.

"That's a good one!" said Miguel, laughing. They shared jokes until their sides hurt—not so much from the jokes but from poking each other in the ribs.

"Why did we stop? Is this Itchy Chicken?" asked Grant when the van jolted to a sudden stop in the middle of the jungle. Enormous green plants sprang up in all directions.

"It's not 'Itchy Chicken,'" corrected Christina from the back seat. "It's pronounced 'chee-chen-eet-za.' And no, we're not there yet!"

"Well, Chichen sounds like chicken, and Itza rhymes with pizza," said Grant. "And, that makes me hungry! Izzy, is this a pit stop for lunch?" he asked.

"Nope, this is no pit stop," said Izzy, "not unless you want to eat with the monkeys! It's just a bit of jungle traffic. A tree fell in the road, that's all."

Izzy slowly maneuvered the van around the fallen tree. Christina heard a tapping noise outside the van. She turned to look. Through the dusty back window, she could make out the shape of a feathered serpent face. It was staring at her with beady eyes.

"Aahhhhh!" screamed Christina. "Go, Izzy, drive! A snake man is trying to get in!" Soon, all the kids were screeching and yelling.

"Quiet down, kids," Izzy said calmly. She adjusted her rear-view mirror. "It's just your overactive imaginations playing tricks on you.

A tall figure with a feathered head scurried back into the jungle. "That was NOT our imagination!" the four yelled in unison.

"Well, it's gone now," Izzy said calmly. "It was probably just a monkey."

The van's motor and the blasting radio were loud enough to muffle the kids' conversation.

Christina and Grant told their new friends about the developing mystery.

"Clues?" asked Eva. "You think all of these things are clues? No wonder your grandmother writes such great stories! She has you two to find mysteries everywhere you go!"

"I never thought about it like that!" exclaimed Grant.

"Well, this jade stone just happens to show up in my backpack—a stone that has the same symbol as the tattoo on Emilio's wrist," said Christina. "Then, when I'm looking for Kayak Man, Emilio just happens to let Grant fall in the water."

"And don't forget about the feathered snake guy that just attacked the van," added Eva.

"Right!" Christina exclaimed.

"And the 365 note back at the hotel," said Grant.

"And the Maya symbols on the back of the stone adding up to 365," added Miguel.

"They've *got* to be clues!" cried Christina. "And something tells me they're leading us to Chichen Itza!"

●●●
___

# 8

# Kukulkan, the Feathered Serpent

"Welcome to the ruins of Chichen Itza!" announced Izzy. "You'll find maps in your seat pockets. There are some really interesting facts on the back!"

The kids piled out of the Lime-O-Zeen. Stretching out in front of them was a large grassy area, and jutting up from the earth stood a huge white pyramid.

   **41**

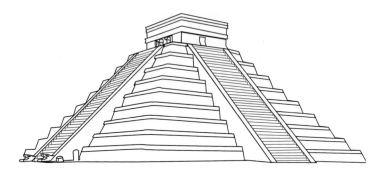

Grant and Miguel immediately ran toward it, dodging tourists along the way. Christina and Eva hurried after them.

"Don't...ever...do...that...again!" huffed and puffed Izzy when she caught up to the kids. "You kids are my responsibility!"

"Sorry, Izzy," Christina apologized. "My brother does this a lot!" She shot Grant an irritated look. "By the way, what does Chichen Itza mean?"

"Maya scholars believe it means 'at the mouth of the well of the water sorcerer'," explained Izzy, still out of breath. "We'll visit the sacred well, or *cenote*, a little later."

"So, who ruined it?" asked Grant.

"Who ruined what?" asked Izzy.

"Chichen Itza," answered Grant. "You said it was ruined."

"Grant, ruins are just the remainders of old buildings or places," Christina explained.

"Right, they're ruined!" said Grant laughing. "And kangaroos did it."

"What?" said the others in unison.

"Yeah, 'roo-ins'—like in 'Kanga-roo-ins'," said Grant.

"There aren't any kangaroos in Mexico," Eva said.

"Sure there are!" chimed in Miguel. "They escaped from the Mexico City Zoo and ruined the pyramid!"

"Not you, too!" cried Eva. Grant and Miguel began to hop around like kangaroos, chanting "Roo-ins! Roo-ins! Roo-ins!"

"Boys, boys!" shouted Izzy, shaking her head. "Follow me. Kangaroos have nothing to do with these ruins."

Grant and Miguel nudged each other in the side, trying to keep from laughing.

"It's gigantic!" exclaimed Christina.

"This is the Temple of Kukulkan," Izzy explained.

"Who or what was Kukul...?" began Christina.

"Kukulkan," Izzy repeated. "Among the Maya, Kukulkan was an important mythological figure—a feathered serpent god," Izzy answered.

"Mythological, mythological," Grant began chanting. Christina cupped her hand over his mouth to stop him.

Izzy continued, "One legend was about Kukulkan as a boy. The boy was born a feathered snake, so his sister had to hide and care for him in a cave. When he grew too big, he flew out of the cave and into the sea. Every July, he causes earthquakes to let his sister know that he is still alive."

Grant and Christina stared at each other in disbelief. "July?" Christina mouthed the word, knowing that it was smack in the middle of July right now.

"The Spanish called the pyramid *El Castillo* when they first saw it. To them it looked like a fortress," Izzy explained. "It was actually a Maya calendar built to honor Kukulkan."

"A calendar?" asked Christina. "But how?"

Izzy pointed at the pyramid. "The four staircases, one on each side of the pyramid, have 91 steps each. Add them up and they equal 364. Then, add the top step, and—"

Christina interrupted Izzy, "You get 365!"

Izzy spotted someone on the lawn and waved him down. "Excuse me, kids, I'll be right back!"

Christina pulled the paper clue out of her pocket and reread it to the others. "365, 91 in 4 directions, a ball of fire warms its top!"

"It's talking about this pyramid," said Grant, "and 91 means the number of steps!"

"And 'in four directions' are the four sides of the pyramid," added Miguel.

"The 'ball of fire' is probably the sun warming the top of the pyramid," said Eva.

Christina finished the last part of the clue. "And '365' is the number of steps in all and the number of days in a year."

Christina looked for Izzy among the tourists milling about the area. Many of them followed tour guides speaking various languages. It was difficult to get a good look at the man Izzy was talking to. But when Christina spotted Izzy, something about her companion seemed familiar. And she noticed that every so often, Izzy stomped her foot and pointed toward the parking lot.

Christina felt for the piece of jade in her pocket. She pulled it out to show everyone. In the sunlight, it was **translucent**. The Mayan symbols on the back lined up perfectly with the serpent head on the front.

Eva said, "I think the snake head on the stone is Kukulkan. Listen to this," she added, pointing to an information display. "It says here that at sunset on the spring and fall equinoxes, the body of Kukulkan moves along the steps of the pyramid until it meets its head at the bottom."

Christina gulped audibly. "It's a good thing it's summer, then!" Snakes, spiders, and bats were not her thing AT ALL.

"Oh, no, Christina, it's just a trick of the light," said Eva. "It says the steps cast a shadow that only *looks* like the body of a giant snake crawling down the stairs."

"Well, that's a relief!" cried Christina.

"Is this Kukulkan's head?" shouted Grant from the base of the pyramid steps where a giant feathered snake head jutted out. Grant fit his head into its stone mouth.

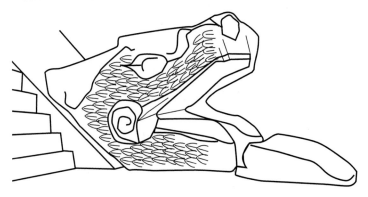

"Grant! It's alive!" Miguel joked.

Grant made a face and screamed like he was being eaten alive. He wiggled his leg in the air for effect.

The movement of Grant's head in the serpent's mouth dislodged a stone. "Ouch!" cried Grant.

Christina yelled, "Get out of there and stop goofing around, Grant!"

"But, Christina, it really is alive! It's shooting stuff at me!" Grant rubbed his head and scowled at the snake head.

"Look!" shouted Christina. "Another piece of jade!" She picked it up and dusted it off. "It must have been hidden in the snake's mouth!"

The kids looked back at Izzy. She was still standing in the middle of the plaza. When she peered back at the kids and waved, she looked quite upset.

"Eva," said Christina, "I think you're right about the jade clue being about Kukulkan!"

●●●●
‾‾‾‾

# 9

# Twisted Snakes

The kids gathered around Christina to study the new jade clue. Like the first piece, it was jagged on two sides. Etched on its surface were two peculiar looking snakes—the bodies were twisted together into a circle until their heads met.

"Gosh, the Maya sure liked snakes— probably as much as I do!" said Grant.

"Let's just hope we don't run into any real snakes on this tour!" said Christina.

She took the first jade piece out of her pocket and fit it together with the second piece.

"They fit like a puzzle!" exclaimed Eva.

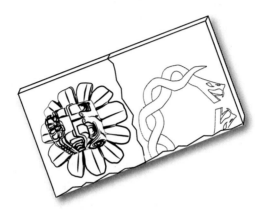

Christina took the twisted snake clue and flipped it over to read the new numbers. "Grant, you are the Maya symbol expert. Help us out."

"Okay," agreed Grant. "There are three numbers this time: 2, 7, and 6."

Christina quickly slipped the stones into her pocket when she saw Izzy approaching.

"Sorry about that, kids," said Izzy. Her face was flushed and she was biting her lip.

"Are you okay?" asked Eva.

"Yes, of course," Izzy answered. "It's just a little hot out here, that's all!"

Christina asked, "Who was that?"

"That guy? Oh, he was just one of my old college professors," Izzy said.

"But, without the fishing hat," mumbled Christina to herself.

"Excuse me?" Izzy said.

"Oh, it's nothing," said Christina. "I just thought he looked familiar—you know, the suit and all."

Izzy seemed caught off guard. "Lots of men wear light cotton suits. It's the style around here in the summer."

Christina scanned the crowd of men and women wearing shorts and jeans. "I guess," she said doubtfully.

"Come on, Miguel," challenged Grant. "Let's see if the Maya really did the math right!"

The boys bolted up the steps of the pyramid's north face. "One, two, three..." they shouted. But, by the fourth step, a guard had grabbed the two boys by their shirt collars. He shouted at them in Spanish to stay off the pyramid.

Izzy apologized to the guard and promised to keep the boys close.

"Boys," Izzy said, gritting her teeth, "you're lucky they didn't throw you in the jail for naughty tourist boys! Tourists aren't allowed to climb the Temple of Kukulkan anymore. It is off limits, understand?" she warned. "Now, I have to make a phone call. I'll be back in a minute." She pulled a candy bar from her back pocket and took a giant bite before heading off in the opposite direction.

She turned back suddenly and said, "Look at your maps and decide where you want to go next. And NO CLIMBING THE PYRAMID!"

Christina motioned the kids into a huddle. "Do the twisted snakes or the numbers 2, 7, and 6 mean anything to you?"

Grant raised his hand.

"Grant, this isn't school, but go ahead," Christina said. "You know what the snakes and numbers mean?"

"Well, I was just wondering if you had any snacks in your backpack," he said. "I think I'm about to pass out from hunger!"

"You're always hungry, Grant," Christina teased.

"Well, I wasn't until I saw Izzy's candy bar!" Grant whined.

Christina pulled out a box of cookies and bottles of water for everyone.

"Thanks for the water and the *bosh* of cookies!" kidded Grant. He giggled and everyone laughed at his joke.

"Christina, stop littering," scolded Grant, motioning toward a piece of paper near her feet. "This is a World Heritage site, after all."

"I wasn't littering! It fell out of my backpack. There's a difference!" Christina said defensively.

She leaned down to pick up the piece of paper and unfolded it. "It's another clue!" whispered Christina excitedly.

*The Mystery at the Maya Ruins*

# 10

# The Eye of the Needle

"Come on!" Christina said. "There are too many people here." The kids sprinted to a quieter corner of the pyramid. Christina unfolded the clue. She read it out loud:

> The eye of a needle in the I fits
> ancient rubber, skulls on sticks.

"I know this one!" cried Grant. "The vendors are selling bubble gum and they have sewing supplies for sale. Come on!"

"Hang on!" Christina said and caught the back of Grant's t-shirt. "What about the skulls on sticks and the letter I?"

"They probably sell those too!" he said.

"There you are!" said Izzy, marching up behind them. "You kids really need to learn to stay in one place! So where are we off to next?" she asked.

"Rubber and skulls?" suggested Christina.

"Oh, you mean the Great Ball Court?" Izzy guessed.

The kids grew wide-eyed. "Yeeeessss!" they said in unison, nodding their heads emphatically. "That's what we mean."

"Hmmm," grunted Izzy, looking the kids up and down.

To their surprise, Izzy tore off running. Her floppy, yellow hat bounced up and down.

It was hard to keep up with her. They could hear her laughing. "Follow me!" she cried.

The gang stood at one end of the Great Ball Court. Carvings depicting scenes from the games were etched along the high walls. Izzy was nowhere in sight.

"Izzy, are you here?" shouted Eva.

"Eva, are you sure this is the Great Ball Court?" Christina asked, opening her map.

"Christina," whispered a voice.

Christina looked around. "Did you hear a voice call my name?"

"I hear Izzy's voice, but I don't see her," said Eva.

"Grant," came the whisper again.

"Izzy, where are you?" shouted Miguel.

"She's got to be here somewhere," said Eva. The group of kids turned in quiet circles.

"Miguel," whispered the voice. "Eva."

Suddenly, a ball came flying hard past Christina's ear. "This isn't funny, Izzy!" Christina cried.

"Ooh, a ball!" said Grant. He chased after it.

In a flash, a colorful feathered serpent came swooshing by the kids. It grabbed Christina's pink backpack.

"My bag!" shouted Christina. "Catch him!"

Thinking quickly, Grant rolled the ball as hard as he could. It crossed the thief's path, causing him to trip and fall. The backpack came free from his grip and skidded to a stop at Eva's feet.

"Got it!" cried Eva.

The thief took off running to the other end of the court.

Just then, they heard a cry.

"Izzy!" they shouted and darted off to find her sitting on the ground, dazed and confused.

"Izzy!" everyone shouted together. "Are you okay?"

"I'm fine," said Izzy. "Some guy in a costume just ran me over!"

"You know, it looked a lot like the feathered serpent guy that tapped on the van window in the jungle!" cried Miguel.

"Now, do you believe us?" Grant asked Izzy.

# 11

# Snakes and Skulls

"Was that you whispering our names earlier?" asked Christina.

Izzy nodded. "Cool trick, huh? I was hiding down there when I whispered your names. For some reason, you can hear a whisper from one end of the court to the other. No one can give me a good explanation as to why, though."

Grant tossed the ball they found high in the air. "This ball is pretty heavy. Do you know what it's made of, Izzy?"

"It's made from the sap of rubber trees," replied Izzy. "Wait! Where did you get that?"

"Maybe it belongs to Feathered Snake Guy," guessed Grant, before throwing the ball and running after it.

"Grant, wait for me!" Christina said, chasing after him.

"Just getting the ball!" he exclaimed. "I think it went up these steps!"

"That's the Temple of the Jaguars," shouted Izzy. "Go on! You can climb that one!"

The temple stood off to the side at one end of the Great Ball Court. The kids raced up the steep outer steps to the second level of the temple. From this height they could look down on the ball court.

"I am King of Itchy Chicken!" roared Grant, opening his arms wide.

"No, I am the king!" hollered Miguel, puffing out his chest.

Grant puffed his chest out, too. "We shall see who is king! Let the games begin!"

"Yes, I agree! Let the games begin!" Miguel echoed.

"Look!" cried Christina. "The I!" She pointed down at the ball court.

*Snakes and Skulls*

"You can see an eyeball from this high up?" asked Grant. "Where?"

"No! The *letter* I—like in the clue!" corrected Christina.

"You're right!" squealed Eva. "The court is in the shape of an I!"

"Cool! Hey, my ball!" shouted Grant. It lay at the base of the steps.

"Hey!" shouted Miguel. "I'm the king! Therefore, it is my ball!"

"Out of my way!" cried Grant. The boys raced down the steps and onto the court below. Eva followed close behind, laughing.

Christina looked out on the ball court. She wondered what it must have been like for girls her age back then. She imagined being a princess.

She pulled out her journal and sketched the ball court. That's when she noticed a round stone with a hole in the middle of it jutting out from the wall high above the ball court.

She raced down the steps. The others met her below the stone ring.

"Look!" she cried. "See that circular rock up there? It has two twisted snakes with their heads meeting at one end."

61

"Just like the carving on the jade stone," said Eva.

Christina agreed and pulled out the latest paper clue.

*The eye of a needle in the I fits ancient rubber, skulls on sticks.*

"The court is in the shape of an I," said Christina.

"This stone ring is probably the eye of the needle," suggested Miguel.

"And the ancient rubber is the ball," guessed Eva.

Izzy limped over to the kids. "Gosh, you really got hurt, didn't you, Izzy?" said Eva. Christina slipped the clue in her pocket before Izzy saw it.

"I'll be fine," she assured them. "This pain doesn't compare to the pain the Maya ball players must have felt. Sometimes the games got pretty brutal!"

"Is that the ball goal up there?" asked Miguel.

"Yes! And there's another one on the other side, too," she said, pointing across the field.

"So, how did the Maya play the game?" asked Grant.

"No rules for the game exist today," Izzy said. "But, from the carvings on the walls of the ball courts, archaeologists believe it was a mix between soccer and basketball. The players scored points by getting the ball through those rings."

"But how? The goals are so high!" exclaimed Christina.

Izzy explained. "The players couldn't use their hands at all, but they could use their feet, knees, and hips. Thick padding helped, but the ball was tossed around with a lot of force. The players sometimes died from getting hit in the stomach or the head!"

"Wow, and I thought playing dodgeball in P.E. was rough!" exclaimed Grant.

"Archaeologists also learned that the ballgames were often seen as being symbolic of battle," Izzy added.

"What about this carving?" asked Christina.

"This carving," Izzy said, "shows two teams of seven players each."

"Oooh, I see snakes coming out of one of them!" cried Christina.

Izzy nodded. "The six snakes represent blood," she explained. "And I have got to sit down," she said, limping off to the shade to let the kids explore.

"Izzy just said the numbers in the clue— 2, 7, and 6!" said Christina. "Two teams, seven players, six bloody snakes!"

"We solved the clue!" said Eva.

"Not quite yet!" said Grant. "I've got an idea. Wait here!" He raced down the court and hopped up on the short end of the wall. Balancing like a tightrope walker, he made it back to just above the goal.

"Grant, what if Izzy sees you?" called Christina.

"Aha!" he said. "Just as I thought—there's another piece of the jade stone!"

Grant heaved the heavy ball he was carrying through the stone ring. It knocked the jade free from its hiding place.

Christina caught the stone mid-air and slipped it into her pocket. It clinked gently against the other two stones.

"That's a goal for Team Grant! Yessss!" he cheered, pumping his fists in the air. When he got down from the wall, he nudged Miguel in the ribs and announced, "I am king—once and for all!"

"OK, OK, you win," Miguel conceded. "You climbed all the way up there, so you get big points for that!"

"Way to score, little brother!" said Christina, patting him on the shoulder.

Christina pulled the jade stones out of her pocket. Together, the kids studied the new piece of the puzzle. On one side was a Mayan number.

"It looks like an eye," said Eva.

"It's not an eye; it's a shell," said Grant. "The shell on the bottom is zero. The dot, or 1, is in the 20's place. So, it's 1 times 20. And 20 plus 0 is 20."

"What would we do without you?!" Christina exclaimed.

"I don't think I've ever heard you say that before!" Grant said.

"And you may never hear that again!" Christina replied with a wink. She turned the jade stone over. "It's an image of a spiral, I think."

"And part of the two snakes, too!" said Miguel.

"It must fit together with the other pieces!" exclaimed Eva.

"Be my guest!" said Christina, handing her friend the stones. Eva carefully placed the three pieces of jade together in a patch of grass.

"A perfect fit!" she said, smiling from ear to ear.

"But," Miguel said, "we still have to figure out the 'skulls on sticks' part of the paper clue!"

"No! No more skulls!" cried Christina.

Izzy approached the kids. Her giant yellow hat flapped like butterfly wings as she walked. Grant plopped down on the jade stones before Izzy could see their treasure.

"I heard someone say they're ready for more skulls! Right this way!" directed Izzy.

*The Mystery at the Maya Ruins*

# 12

# Walls and Wells

"Welcome to the Wall of Skulls," Izzy announced. "This is where the ancient Maya performed human sacrifices. It's gruesome, but true," she added.

"Hey, Grant, check out the carvings of the skulls on this wall," Miguel said.

"Whoa! It's like Halloween year 'round here!" Grant exclaimed.

Izzy spoke. "Archaeologists believe that sacrifices were performed on this platform. Then, the skulls were put on poles!"

The skulls-on-sticks clue was just solved, but that didn't make Christina feel any better. All the talk of skulls on poles was making Christina feel woozy. She leaned against the wall and fanned herself with her map.

Suddenly, the hair on the back of her neck rose. Something touched her shoulder. She whipped around and came face to face with a skull carving.

"Aahhhhhhhh!" screamed Christina. Laughter erupted from behind the wall. Grant popped up. "Boo!" he shouted.

"I'll get you for that!" Christina yelled and chased her brother down a long dirt path to a roped-off area surrounding a giant water hole. Grant nearly fell into it, but his sister caught his shirt before toppling over herself. The pair grasped at vines and exposed roots along the face of the **chasm** to keep from sliding into the pea-soup-green water below.

"It's a good thing no one saw you two!" chided Izzy, as she pulled the siblings away from the well.

"It's a good thing this giant hole is only halfway filled!" gasped Christina as she brushed the dirt off her clothes.

"This is actually a sacred well, or *Cenote Sagrado* in Spanish," said Izzy. "Scientists say there are no rivers and very few lakes on the Yucatan Peninsula because of the limestone everywhere. All of the water is underground. Occasionally, though, the ground will give way and cause a sinkhole. The water underground rises into these sinkholes, making a waterhole, or well, that the Maya called a *cenote*."

"So, this isn't a manmade well?" asked Grant.

"No, it's a natural water hole. It was used by the Maya for a very long time," Izzy explained. "In times of drought, Maya from all around would visit this *cenote* to offer sacrifices to the rain god, Chac."

"Sacrifices?" Christina gulped.

"Yes," Izzy replied. "Archaeologists know this because thousands of items, like shells and gold and jade, and even wood, have been pulled out of here."

"Oh, and it says here—bones, too!" added Grant, reading the back of his map.

Izzy cringed. "Yes, even bones," she admitted.

"Bones? Again?!" cried Christina. "And I almost fell in there!"

"Yes!" joked Grant. "A few more feet and we would have been toast for the rain god!"

"Don't worry, they removed all the bones!" Izzy said gently. "The Maya believed that some of these wells were magical portals to the underworld."

BZZZ! BZZZ! BZZZ! It was Izzy's cell phone. "Hang on, kids. I'll be right back." Izzy plopped down on a fallen tree trunk.

Grant and Miguel snuck up behind Christina and Eva. "What are we whispering about now?" whispered Grant. Christina and Eva jumped.

"Don't sneak up on us like that, Grant!" cried Christina. "All this talk of sacrifices and bones and skulls on poles has me a little on edge!"

"Like on the edge of that waterhole, right?" Grant joked.

"Ha ha!" said Christina. "Do you still have the jade stones?"

Grant reached into his pocket and pulled out a fuzzy gumball, a receipt for a slingshot he bought but lost, and some leftover cookies from their snack. "I put the jade stones in my pocket, but now they're not here!" cried Grant.

The kids all turned to look into the sacred well. "No way!" cried Christina. "I just can't go in there! Not, with all the bones and stuff at the bottom!"

"Christina, all of the bones have been removed, remember?" said Eva.

"Yeah, that's just what they tell you to make you feel better!" she cried.

"What's a few bones, anyway?" asked Grant and jumped into the water feet first.

"Grant, no!" yelled Christina. "The bones!"

Izzy ran over to the kids. "What on earth is your little brother up to now? My story didn't scare him one bit, did it?"

Telling Izzy about the jade stones didn't seem right to Christina, so she got brave. Before jumping in after her brother, she cried, "Just going in for a swim, that's all!"

"Not you, too!" Izzy cried.

"Yeah, that's what we're doing. Whew! What a warm day," said Miguel and jumped in, too, followed by his sister.

"Kids, the *Cenote Sagrado* is off limits to tourists!" Izzy called after them.

After their quick dip, Grant, Miguel, and Eva climbed up the steep bank of the water hole with no problem. But Christina couldn't manage to get a good foothold in the roots. The side of the waterhole crumbled under her, sending her down a few feet.

"I can't watch anymore!" cried Izzy, as she moved away from the waterhole. "Grant and Miguel, come over here. Will you help Christina? And Grant, please don't fall in again, okay?"

The boys got on their stomachs and reached down to pull Christina up the ledge when she got close enough. Izzy was on the lookout for anyone who might catch them in the sacred waterhole.

"Did you find the stones in the water?" Grant whispered to Christina.

"Nope!" Christina answered. "But, I found this!" She showed them a note she found clinging to a branch on her way up.

The note was soaking wet but they could still read the words. In the same scrawled handwriting as the first two clues, the note said:

Coils rise to reveal a sparkly blanket above.

# 13

# A Portal to the Underworld!

"How would a clue get all the way down there?" wondered Eva out loud.

Just then, a flash of white jumped out from behind a nearby bush, ripped the note from Christina's hand, and dove into the *cenote*. The man's jacket got caught on a bush as he went in, ripping the pocket. His wallet plunked into the dirt.

Christina picked it up and looked over the edge. There was no sign of the mystery man.

"He's still under there!" Christina whimpered. "And with all those bones, too!"

"Who was that?" asked Grant. He hopped on one foot to dislodge the water from his ears.

"We're about to find out!" Christina said. Inside the man's wallet was a card with the symbol of a feathered serpent! The card looked like it had been torn in half and taped back together. "It looks like he belongs to some secret club!"

Tucked in the window of the wallet was a university badge with a photo of a man with a distinctive mole on his cheek. It was hard to make out the man's name.

"I know that guy!" Grant whispered. "He was at the antique shop."

Just then, Izzy approached the kids and snatched the wallet from Christina's hand.

"I'll take that," she said, "and pass it on to the authorities, of course." She dropped it into her handbag. "They know how to deal with thieves."

Christina waited until Izzy left. "It was the same guy at the antique shop? Are you sure, Grant?"

"Yes, I got a really good look at him through his magnifying glass as he was studying the stone at the shop," replied Grant.

*A Portal to the Underworld!*

"That means he's been following us since Cozumel!" cried Christina.

"He must have slipped the stone into your backpack!" said Grant.

"And then followed us out on the kayak!" Christina cried.

"The stone must be very important to him," noted Miguel.

"If it was that important to him, he shouldn't have put it in my bag!" Christina exclaimed.

Christina looked back at the well. There was still no sign of the man. "Maybe that stuff Izzy was saying about the *cenote* being a portal to the underworld is true!" she yelped.

"He must have gotten out. There's a lot of brush way over there on the other side of the waterhole," said Eva.

"I just wish he'd leave us alone!" cried Christina.

"The jade!" shouted Grant. He was standing behind the girls.

"I know, Grant!" Christina sighed. "Now that the clue is gone, we'll never find the last jade stone!"

"No, the jade stones—they were in my other pocket!" said Grant, handing them back to Christina.

"You mean we went into that sacrificial well for nothing?!" Christina cried.

"Not for nothing!" Grant said. "You found that clue about 'coils rising to reveal the sparkly blanket,' remember?"

"You remember the clue?" Christina cried. "Thank goodness! I thought it was lost forever! I forgive you for making me go swimming in that creepy waterhole!"

"I'll tell you what's creepy!" whispered Grant. "Izzy just called the guy in the white suit the thief. The guy in white isn't the thief. That's the serpent guy. Why would she think they're the same person?"

"I have no idea!" said Christina.

"I think he's the same guy that upset Izzy in the plaza," said Eva. "He was wearing a shiny white suit then, too."

"But, if that's the case, Eva, Izzy knows who's behind all of this!" said Miguel.

*A Portal to the Underworld!*

"Then, I take it back," said Eva. "Because that would mean Izzy is involved in all this mystery craziness! I just can't believe that!"

"Yeah, you're probably right," said Christina.

*But deep down inside, Christina had her doubts—especially now. When Izzy grabbed the wallet, part of a red-feathered serpent tattoo on her shoulder peeked out from under her sleeveless shirt.*

# 14

# The Sparkling Blanket

"I'm hungry!" grumbled Grant.

"I'm thirsty!" complained Miguel.

"Sorry, guys! We're out of food and water," said Christina.

"Kids," said Izzy, "there's a vendor by the observatory. We can grab something there. Then, after a quick peek in the observatory, we'll be ready for the big light show this evening!"

"Yay!" cried the kids.

"There's no moon tonight," she warned, "so it'll be very dark. You have to promise to stick together, OK?"

"OK!" everyone promised.

Eva said, "It says here that during the light show, the buildings all light up in different colors as they talk about the history of Chichen Itza."

"By the time the show is over, won't it be too late to drive back?" asked Miguel between chewy bites of a delicious Barrita, a fruit-filled cookie.

"Yes, it will," said Izzy. "So, we'll be camping at a place about a mile from here. They rent out hammocks."

"Outside?" asked Christina. "Like with the monkeys, spiders, and snakes?"

"Yes, outside," repeated Izzy.

"Christina, remember that saying, 'When in Italy, eat pizza like you are in Mexico'? No, that's not it. It's 'When eating pizza in Mexico, act like a Roman.' No, wait, I know, it's 'When in a Roman pizza parlor—'"

"Grant!" Christina interrupted. "I get it. OK, I'll go."

"Then that's settled," said Izzy. "Go check out the observatory. I'll throw the trash away."

"I'll race you!" shouted Christina. The kids sprinted up the stairs to the ancient dome-shaped building and stopped at the entrance.

"This is the Caracol Observatory," said Christina, reading the back of the map.

"It says the Maya built it to track astronomical events, like equinoxes and eclipses," added Eva.

"Wow! They tracked 20 of the possible 29 astronomical events from this observatory!" exclaimed Christina.

"What are we waiting for?" shouted Grant. "Maybe we'll see an eclipse!"

The kids ran inside.

"Look, everyone! There's a spiral staircase!" cried Miguel.

"The clues!" cried Eva. "It makes sense now! A *caracol* is a snail in Spanish! At first, I thought the coils in the clue were of a snake. But they have to mean the coiling stairs—like a coiled snail shell."

"The jade stone clue had a spiral on it!" said Christina. "It must mean this spiral staircase, too!"

"And the sparkly blanket from the paper clue has to be the night sky," said Miguel.

"What about the Maya number 20?" asked Grant.

"Remember," Christina said, "that's the number of astronomical events the Maya could see from this observatory."

The kids climbed the observatory stairs and stopped at the top. The wind blew through the openings in the top of the dome. It made an eerie whistling sound.

"The Maya had a beautiful view of the night sky," said Christina.

"I was just thinking," Grant said. "The jade stones led us to other jade stones, right?"

"Yes," agreed Christina.

"So, why are there note clues, too?" asked Grant.

"I guess it's in case we miss one of the jade clues," said Christina.

"Then, who's leaving the clues?" he asked. "It can't be the feathered snake guy. He keeps trying to get the jade stones back. If it's White Suit, then why leave clues and then steal them back?"

"You have a point, little brother," said Christina.

Christina pulled the stones out and set them down on a ledge in the observatory. One by one, she arranged the stone pieces. "One piece to go," she observed.

The sun set in the west with a burst of pinks and purples that seemed to settle on the ruins. The sky was sprinkled with stars.

"There! You can see Venus!" Christina pointed through a slit in the dome.

"Imagine," said Eva excitedly, "we're standing in the same place the Maya did when they saw the planet centuries ago!"

"Stand back!" said Miguel. "Look!"

    **87**

As the light of Venus filtered through the fourth slit in the roof of the observatory, it stopped and hovered over the three pieces of jade resting on the ledge. Then, like a finger, the light began to trace the images etched on each stone, beginning with the first and ending with the third.

"It's reading the stones!" cried Grant.

Suddenly, a beam of light shot out of the third stone and pierced a point on the wall, causing a part of the wall to open up.

"The fourth jade piece!" cried Christina. There, in the recess of the wall, was the missing piece of jade.

The face of a jaguar was etched on the front. The back of the stone was completely smooth. Suddenly, the dome ceiling above them burst into color just as the sun disappeared below the horizon.

"What's happening?" cried Christina. She grabbed the stones and slid them all into her backpack.

"The dome! It wants the stone back!" gasped Grant.

*The Sparkling Blanket*

The kids practically stumbled over each other as they descended the spiral stairwell.

"Izzy!" Grant yelled. "Run for your life! The observatory is about to blow!"

# 15

# Timberrrrrr!

Realizing that he was alone, Grant stopped running and turned around. He saw a bright white cellphone light floating in front of the brightly lit Caracol Observatory—and pointed right at him!

"Grant," said Christina, wiggling her cellphone light as she caught up to him, "the observatory isn't going to blow! It's just the light show. It's already begun!"

"Ohhhh! Oops!" Grant said.

"Let's head to the light show!" said Izzy. "Remember, stick with me—no matter what!" she warned.

The gang moved close to the pyramid, where the crowd had grown since the morning. Families with small kids were settled on blankets. Everyone watched the history of Chichen Itza unfold before their eyes. A smooth dialog of Spanish floated over the loudspeaker.

Grant stood mesmerized as the pyramid lit up. With a trick of the lighting, the ghostly shape of Kukulkan appeared to descend the side of the pyramid to meet his head at the base of the steps. Applause from the crowd was deafening.

Following the light show, the crowd of people began to leave the ruins. The four kids lingered near the pyramid while Izzy spoke with several tourists about the history of the ruins.

All of a sudden, the ground rumbled and shifted, causing the kids to lose their balance and fall to their knees.

"TIMBERRRRRR!" shouted Grant.

"That's no tree falling," shouted Christina. "That's an earthquake!"

The kids crawled to the side of the pyramid and leaned against the wall for balance. The ground rumbled for only about ten seconds, but it felt like forever. Izzy was swept away in a crowd of tourists running toward the parking lot.

"Izzy!" screamed Eva.

"She can't hear us," cried Christina. "She's too far away!"

"I guess this means Kukulkan is still alive and well!" exclaimed Grant.

"I guess so," Christina agreed.

POP! SCREEEEECH!

Christina yelped, "What was that?" She turned to see a steel door behind them. "Look, the lock to the pyramid! It's broken!" she said, shining her light on the door. She pushed it open.

"There's an entrance to the inside?" asked Grant. "Why didn't anyone tell me?"

Izzy came running from the parking lot and cried, "I saw your cellphone light, Christina. Thank goodness you kids stayed put this time!"

"Yes! No one's hurt," Christina said.

"We should go now. Aftershocks always follow earthquakes!" warned Izzy. "Christina, where's Grant?"

"Oh no! He's gone!" Christina cried.

*The Mystery at the Maya Ruins*

# 16

# Echoes and Chirps

"He must have gone inside," said Miguel.

"The pyramid is open?" Izzy asked, shocked. "But it hasn't been open to the public for years!"

"The earthquake broke the lock!" Christina said. "Come on!"

The kids followed Christina through the metal door and up the steep steps at the entrance of the pyramid.

The air was stifling. It was pitch-black inside, except for the small beacon of light coming from Christina's phone.

Izzy stood at the entrance, protesting, but no one heard. "Wait for me!" she called.

"Grant!" Christina shouted.

"It's so dark in here," yelped Eva. She turned on her own cellphone for light.

"I hope we don't run into any spiders, or worse—snakes!" cried Christina.

"Christina!" It was Grant's voice.

"Grant?" called Christina.

"Over here!" answered Grant.

"He's behind this wall," said Miguel. He began tapping on it.

"Grant, don't worry! We'll get you out!" Christina cried. "Miguel, give me your shoe!"

"I'm right here." Grant popped out from behind the wall.

"Grant! We thought you were trapped behind one of those spinning walls!" cried Christina.

"They have those here?" asked Grant.

"Kids, let's get out of here!" commanded Izzy. Cellphone lights danced like fireflies. "Stop moving!" she yelled.

"Ouch! I hit my knee on something!" Grant cried.

"You just ran into a chac mool," Izzy said. She pointed to a reclining stone figure leaning back on its elbows.

"Why is it lying back like that?" asked Eva.

"It was used for sacrificial offerings to the gods," she explained.

"Look at this!" Grant shouted from the other end of the chamber.

The group circled around a statue of a jaguar. It was painted red and had bright green jade spots inlaid in its body.

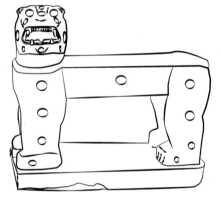

"It's amazing!" cried Christina and clapped her hands.

"That's the Jaguar Throne," Izzy began. She was interrupted by the sound of a bird chirping. "Is that a bird? How peculiar!" mumbled Izzy. "If you clap *outside* the pyramid, the echo sounds like the Quetzal—a sacred mythological bird." She clapped her hands. A bird echoed back again.

"Oh, how cool!" said Grant.

"It sounded like it came from over there," Izzy mumbled. She used her cellphone to go deeper into the pyramid. The kids could still hear Izzy clapping as she turned around a stone corner.

CLAP....CHIRP....CLAP....CHIRP

"Look, here!" said Grant. "One of the spots on the Jaguar Throne is missing! Christina, the stones!"

Christina placed the jade stones into the missing jaguar spot one piece at a time. Each new piece she added to the jaguar glowed a bright green.

After Christina put three of the stones into the statue, the kids heard a muffled cry.

"That was Izzy! Let's go!" shouted Christina.

The kids took off in the direction of the cry and found Izzy crouched in a dark corner.

"Izzy! Are you okay?" asked Christina.

"Yes, I am," she said, "but my cellphone battery died."

Crawling down the wall behind Izzy's head was a hairy spider the size of Christina's hand. It extended one of its hairy legs and touched Izzy's shoulder.

Eva screeched and jumped up and down, making the shadow of the spider seem to do the same.

"Don't move, Izzy!" Christina warned. "There's a spider behind you!"

Izzy froze. The spider crawled across her back and up onto her yellow floppy hat.

"Get it off me!" squealed Izzy.

"Eva, give me some light!" Christina whispered.

Very carefully, Christina reached over and grabbed the two sides of Izzy's hat. She lifted it off her head and set it on the floor.

"Let's get out of here!" cried Izzy.

"What about your hat?" cried Christina. "We can't leave it in here!"

"I'll get it," said Miguel bravely. He flicked the spider off and ran back with the others to the inner chamber.

When they all got back to the inner chamber, Christina looked around and said, "Wait, where's Grant? NOT AGAIN!"

Suddenly, the floor pitched and swung, forcing the kids against the walls of the chamber.

"Whoa!" cried Miguel. "That was a powerful aftershock!"

"Kids!" shouted Izzy. "We have to go now! It's too dangerous!"

"But what about Grant?" shouted Christina. "The spider will get him!"

"Don't worry, Christina," Izzy cried. "He's probably already outside!"

# 17

# Trail of Feathers

Outside, the earth was still. The plaza was deserted. A few cars, including Izzy's Lime-O-Zeen, were still in the parking lot.

"I don't see Grant anywhere!" cried Christina. "What's that, Miguel?" Eva asked.

"This? It's a feather." Miguel said. "I found it next to the Jaguar Throne."

"May I?" Christina asked, taking the feather from Miguel and holding it up to her light.

"It looks like the feathers from the feathered serpent that attacked us in the Great Ball Court!" Izzy cried. She sounded angry.

"Look, there're more!" shouted Miguel. He pointed to a trail of feathers. A gust of wind began to toss them in different directions.

"We're losing the trail!" shouted Christina. "Come on!"

The trail stopped in front of tall columns. The rock pillars stood erect and still like soldiers blanketed in darkness.

"Grant!" called Christina. "Are you here?"

"This is the Temple of the Thousand Columns!" said Izzy.

Christina's eyes began to adjust to the dark. "There are so many of them! We'll never find him!" she cried.

"Why would your brother take off like that?" asked Izzy.

"I doubt he'd run off this late at night, unless someone were chasing him," Christina replied.

Christina could make out the shapes of Miguel and Eva. Eva's cell phone lit their path. "Any luck?" Christina called to her friends.

"Not yet!" Eva answered. "There's another set of columns. We'll go check there."

"Be careful!" Christina warned. "The feathered snake man is still on the loose!"

"We will!" the kids promised. She listened to them call her brother's name until their voices grew faint and she thought she could hear her own heart beating.

The sound of tires squealing in the distance broke the silence. Christina hoped that was Feathered Snake Guy leaving for good.

Christina didn't completely trust Izzy, but she was worried about her brother. She decided to tell Izzy everything. She left out the part about finding the three other pieces of jade until she knew Izzy could be trusted.

Izzy began to laugh.

"What's so funny?" asked Christina.

"I promised my aunt, Professor Z, that I wouldn't say anything because it was her idea," Izzy said. "But, under the circumstances—"

"What?" Christina interrupted.

"The clues were part of the tour," she admitted.

Christina was speechless.

"I must say, you kids are **tenacious**—never giving up, no matter what!" she remarked. "Most kids don't even find the clues, much less know what to do with them."

"Well," Christina said, "it might have something to do with the fact that we have a grandmother who writes mystery books!"

"Well, actually, your grandparents were in on it, too!" exclaimed Izzy.

"That doesn't surprise me!" Christina laughed and asked, "Are the guy in the white suit and the feathered snake guy part of the tour, too?"

Izzy grew serious. "Christina, there's something you need to know."

"Does it have anything to do with your tattoo? Emilio has one, too," Christina said.

"Oh, you noticed?" she asked, adjusting her shirt around her shoulder. "Yes, actually, it does," Izzy admitted.

Izzy told Christina about how her secret club, the Feathered Serpents, works to preserve the Maya culture. She revealed that one of the members, Dr. Angelo, a professor at the university and a man of many costumes, had lost sight of their mission. She explained that he had become obsessed with collecting rare artifacts for himself instead of protecting them.

"OK, so White Suit and Feathered Snake Guy are the same person? And he belongs in this secret club of yours, right?" Christina asked.

"Well, not any more," admitted Izzy.

"So, Dr. Angelo went rogue. But if you thought he was up to no good, then why didn't you stop him?" asked Christina.

"Believe me, I tried!" Izzy exclaimed.

"We think he's after this," said Christina, handing Izzy the fourth jade stone. "Grant remembers him from the antique shop. We think he put the stone in my bag then."

"A jade stone? And all this time, I thought he was following me around because we kicked him out of the Feathered Serpent Club!" Izzy said.

"But why would he put this in my bag?" asked Christina.

"This must be the stone from the legend! Dr. Angelo knew how important this stone was. He probably didn't want to be seen buying it from the shop. There would be a record of his purchase," Izzy explained.

"Wait, what legend?" Christina asked.

"I didn't think it was true, but Dr. Angelo became obsessed with it! It's like he became a completely different person," Izzy began. "Well, it's an ancient Maya legend. Long ago, in Chichen Itza, the high priest had a vision that among them were hidden four pieces of the same stone. The prophecy foretold that great riches would befall the one who finds the stones and reveals its treasure."

Christina's eyes grew wide.

"Is there more?" shouted Grant.

"Grant?!" cried Christina.

"Up here!" he shouted back.

On top of one of the tall warrior columns sat Grant, cross-legged and smiling.

# 18

# 18 Generations of Sadness

"I guess you followed my feather trail, huh?" he said and slid down the tall stone column.

"Wow! Great hiding place, Grant!" Christina cried. "If I weren't so happy to see you, I'd punch you in the arm."

"Gosh, Christina, if the legend hadn't been so interesting, I'd be mad right now that you're not trying very hard to find me!" Grant shot back.

"Well, if you—!" Christina began.

"Kids!" shouted Izzy. "Grant, tell us what happened! Why did you take off like that?"

"Well," Grant said, "I thought I'd go find the mythological bird myself."

"It wasn't really a bird, Grant," said Izzy. "It was just an echo that sounds like a bird because I clapped."

"That's what I thought, too, but it wasn't a bird at all. Although he did have feathers like a bird..." Grant trailed off.

"Graaaaant!" shouted Christina.

"Oh, right! It wasn't a bird after all," Grant said. "It was that feathered snake guy! He tried to trick me into giving him the jade stones!"

"Stones!" cried Izzy. "There's more than one?"

Christina looked down at her feet.

"You found the other three pieces here in Chichen Itza?" asked Izzy. She sounded impressed.

"Yes, we did," admitted Christina. "Each of the pieces was a clue to find the next one." Then, Christina asked Grant, "You didn't give the stones to Feathered Snake Guy, did you?"

    108

"No! I didn't have them," he said, sounding offended. "I kicked him in the shin and yanked feathers off his costume. Then, I made a run for it!"

"So, the legend could be true?" asked Izzy breathlessly. "Christina, I wasn't finished telling you the legend!" She looked around. "Where are the others?"

"They'll be here soon," said Christina. "I just texted Eva."

When Eva and Miguel returned, Izzy started the legend from the beginning.

"So," said Izzy, coming to the end of the legend, "the legend did foretell of great riches for the person who finds all four stones, but it also warned that 18 generations of great sadness would follow!"

"The jade stones! We left them in the pyramid!" Christina cried.

"We have to get them!" exclaimed Izzy. "Those stones could be very dangerous. We can't risk anyone getting their hands on them!"

The kids were relieved to find the jade still resting in the Jaguar Throne. Christina removed the three stones one by one from the Jaguar Throne and placed them on top of the statue.

"So, they fit together?" asked Izzy.

"Yes," said Christina. "Like a puzzle!"

The kids watched as Izzy arranged the pieces. When she placed the last piece with the other three, the stones glowed bright green, filling the chamber with its soft light.

"It's here! The treasure is here! I can feel it!" gasped Izzy.

The kids looked at one another and then back at Izzy. Something was different about Izzy. Her eyes were darker and a strange smile crept across her lips.

Christina reached for the stones, but Izzy grabbed her arm. "I have to know if the legend is true! This is every archaeologist's dream!" she cried.

Izzy grabbed the jade pieces, and before the kids could stop her, she placed the pieces back into the missing spot on the Jaguar Throne.

The floor began to rumble beneath their feet. Bright pins of light sprang from the bottom of the jaguar and shot to the ceiling of the pyramid. The Jaguar Throne began to rotate.

At exactly ninety degrees, the statue stopped, revealing mounds of jewels. Gold, jade, rubies, and diamonds sparkled brilliantly in a secret chamber below the statue.

Izzy began to laugh, softly at first. Then, her laugh grew louder and louder until the kids had to cover their ears. Christina knew Izzy had changed. She knew they had to do something to stop Izzy from taking the treasure herself and losing everything she believed in. Christina looked at Grant and nodded.

As Christina held Izzy back, Grant removed the jade stones from the Jaguar Throne.

"No!" cried Izzy. "The treasure!"

"Sorry, Izzy," said Grant, "but you're forgetting about the 18 generations of sadness that will follow. That sounds like an awful long time to me! I don't think I can wait that long to feel happy again."

The Jaguar Throne rumbled into place, and they were thrown back into darkness.

Outside the pyramid, Izzy rubbed her eyes and shook her head as if waking from a trance.

"What just happened?" asked Izzy, as if coming out of a daze.

"The real Izzy's back!" they cried happily.

In the parking lot, they stopped a park official as the group was getting into Izzy's Lime-O-Zeen. They told him the lock on the pyramid door appeared broken and that he should check it out. The guard thanked them profusely and ran toward the pyramid.

Grant secretly handed the kids one jade piece each. "Just to be safe," he whispered.

MEOW...MEOW...MEOW!

"Hey, I think you have another passenger, Izzy. I just heard a cat," said Miguel.

"No, it's a text from Mimi," Christina said, pulling out her phone. "It says, 'Come back pronto! You OK?'"

Christina quickly answered Mimi's text.

*On our way now! Survived the earthquake without a scratch! Thanks for texting—I was NOT looking forward to sleeping in a hammock in the jungle tonight!*

*The Mystery at the Maya Ruins*

# 19

# Oliver's Been Shark-Napped!

Izzy plugged her phone into the Lime-O-Zeen charger. After a few seconds, her phone blinked to life. Missed phone and text messages began popping up.

"There's a long message from my aunt," said Izzy.

"From Grandmother?" asked Eva. "I just texted her back to say we're on our way."

"These are from earlier today, when my phone died," said Izzy. "She says that it's as if

Oliver has disappeared from the face of the planet!"

"Oliver's gone?" cried Eva. "Where would a whale shark hide?"

"She says she's not getting any signal from the tracking device," explained Izzy.

"Maybe the tracking device is a dud. I know that happens with firecrackers all the time," said Grant.

Christina received a text from Mimi. She said, "Mimi and Papa are meeting us in Chiquila since the ferries don't run this late."

BZZZ! BZZZ! BZZZ!

"It's a video text from Angelo!" gasped Izzy.

The video began with a close-up of Oliver and then panned out. The bottom of Professor Z's boat was visible. Swim fins disappeared from the water two at a time.

"That's us getting out of the water and being pulled into the boat!" said Miguel.

The video turns away from the boat. "Look!" cried Christina. "Oliver is coming back—and fast!"

The video went black.

"But, why would Dr. Angelo send you a video of Oliver?" asked Grant.

"I have no idea, Grant," said Izzy. "But it can't be good! Wait! It's another text from him."

"Another video?" asked Christina.

"No. It's worse! It's a ransom note!" Izzy cried. "Read this!"

Izzy handed her phone to Christina. Christina read the message. "36527620. Look familiar? The four stones for Oliver, or else!"

"Do you think Dr. Angelo has shark-napped Oliver?" cried Grant.

"Those are the numbers from the jade stones!" exclaimed Christina.

Izzy exclaimed, "Oh no! It's all my fault!"

"How is any of this your fault, Izzy?" asked Christina.

"The legend spoke of random Maya numbers," she explained.

"The ones on the stones!" noted Christina.

"Yes, but, without the actual pieces of jade, the numbers had no meaning to us," Izzy said.

"What does this have to do with Oliver?" asked Christina.

"Dr. Angelo must have overheard me and my aunt talking about using those numbers in the code for the tracking device," explained Izzy. "I've made such a mess of things!"

"No, Dr. Angelo has!" said Grant.

Izzy read her text out loud as she wrote it. "Where... have...you...put...Oliver?"

BZZZ! BZZZ! BZZZ!

"He wrote back!" cried Izzy. "He says, 'For now, the signal to Oliver's tracking device is only scrambled, so no one can find him. But, heed my warning! The stones for Oliver—or else!'"

"We don't have a choice," cried Eva.

"That's out of the question!" said Izzy. "Remember the legend?"

"Well, what if we only let him think he's getting the stones?" suggested Grant. "We'll arrange a drop-off and give him fake stones!"

"Great plan, Grant!" Christina said. "I'm sure we can find some fake jade stones in a gift shop. And I'm so glad Oliver hasn't been kidnapped—he's just had his tracking device scrambled!"

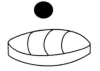

# 20

# A Gift to Kukulkan

That night, at the town of Chiquila, the group met Mimi and Papa on the docks. "On the boat ride over, the strangest thing happened," said Mimi. "Oliver came to say hello!"

Papa added, "He bumped the boat so hard that we thought it was an earthquake!"

Grant said, "He probably just wanted to let everyone know he was alive and well—just like in the legend of Kukulkan!"

"Izzy taught you well!" laughed Professor Z. "Anyone interested in going out on the boat tomorrow morning?"

**119**

The kids could hardly contain their excitement. "Maybe we'll see Oliver again!"

The next morning, as the boat sped through the Caribbean Sea, Izzy asked Grant, "Do you have the stones?"

"You already asked me that twice back at the marina," Grant said, patting his pocket.

"What if the plan doesn't work?" asked Miguel.

"What if he figures out Emilio put another tracking device on Oliver early this morning?" asked Eva.

"Kids, don't worry. My aunt hasn't activated the device yet, so Dr. Angelo won't know," said Izzy.

"But, if Oliver already has a new tracking device on him, why are we doing this?" asked Miguel.

Christina said, "As long as Oliver is feeding in this area, he's in danger, right, Izzy?"

"That's right. We need to keep Dr. Angelo distracted until Oliver migrates from here," Izzy explained.

The kids were sad that Oliver wasn't in his normal feeding spot when they anchored the boat.

"At least we know he's safe," noted Eva.

"We should enjoy ourselves while we're here," suggested Grant. They took turns jumping off the side of the boat and playing tag in the water until they spotted Dr. Angelo's kayak. Like before, he was wearing a shiny white suit and a fishing hat. But instead of waving, he had a snarl on his face.

"I think he figured out that the stones we left at the drop-off were fake stones! Now, what are we going to do?" cried Christina.

"Hey, where's your chicken suit?" shouted Grant to Dr. Angelo. The comment only made the man angrier. He rowed furiously through the water toward the boat.

Christina looked up. Professor Z, Mimi, and Papa were talking on the boat's upper deck, unaware of what was happening below them.

Eva pointed at Dr. Angelo. "He's too close!" she squealed.

Just then, a giant shadow moved through the water and rose to the surface. It headed in the direction of the kayak.

"Oliver!" cried Izzy and the kids.

Professor Z, accompanied by Mimi and Papa, rushed down when they heard Oliver's name.

"Look!" cried Grant. "Oliver has a grudge."

They all watched as Oliver bumped the kayak with his nose and sent Dr. Angelo sprawling into the water. Dr. Angelo surfaced, clutching his fishing hat and sputtering salt water. The flipped-over kayak quickly bubbled and sank beneath the waves.

"A little help, please?" cried Dr. Angelo.

"You'll get some help, all right, when we turn you in to the authorities for tampering with our scientific devices," said Izzy triumphantly. Christina and Grant cheered.

"OK, OK!" Dr. Angelo sputtered as the kids prepared to drag him into the boat. "Just don't leave me out here with that whale shark!"

As the boat zoomed through the water, Izzy formally invited the kids to join the Feathered Serpent Club. To show that she was serious, she put red feathered serpent tattoos on each of their wrists.

"The tattoos may be temporary," Izzy said, "but your membership in the club is forever!"

Christina felt proud to be a part of something so important.

As the boat zipped across the water, the kids took turns tossing their jade into the sea. To honor the Maya, they timed their throws for every 365 seconds.

"The last one is for you, Kukulkan!" shouted Grant. "May you shake the Earth every July!"

For a split second, as the stones flew through the air, the jade glowed bright green, before dipping into the waves and settling to the bottom of the sea.

# The End

# About the Author

Carole Marsh is an author and publisher who has written many works of fiction and non-fiction for young readers. She travels throughout the United States and around the world to research her books. In 1979, Carole Marsh was named Communicator of the Year for her corporate communications work with major national and international corporations.

Marsh is the founder and CEO of Gallopade International, established in 1979. Today, Gallopade International is widely recognized as a leading source of educational materials for every state and many countries. Marsh and Gallopade were recipients of the 2004 Teachers' Choice Award. Marsh has written more than 50 Carole Marsh Mysteries™. In 2007, she was named Georgia Author of the Year. Years ago, her children, Michele and Michael, were the original characters in her mystery books. Today, they continue the Carole Marsh Books tradition by working at Gallopade. By adding grandchildren Grant and Christina as new mystery characters, she has continued the tradition for a third generation.

Ms. Marsh welcomes correspondence from her readers. You can e-mail her at fanclub@gallopade.com, visit carolemarshmysteries.com, or write to her in care of Gallopade International, P.O. Box 2779, Peachtree City, Georgia, 30269 USA.

# Built-In Book Club

# Talk About It!

1. The actions of a character in a story can change the story completely. For example, by running off at the beginning of the story, Grant caused the family to miss their cruise ship. Discuss other actions by characters in the story that affected what happened next.

2. Grant does and says a lot of funny things in tense or scary situations. Talk about specific events like this in the story.

3. Numbers play an important role in the mystery. Discuss your favorite number, or set of numbers, and explain why you liked it.

4. The ball in the story is important in several ways. Discuss the various ways Grant uses the ball and how his actions move the story along.

5. Discuss the choice Grant and Christina made in the pyramid when they noticed Izzy had changed. Talk about what the kids did and what Grant said to Izzy to explain his actions. Do you think you would have made the same choice?

6. What did the kids do with the jade stone pieces at the end of the mystery? Discuss whether they made the right decision and why.

7. Izzy inducts the kids into the Feathered Serpent Club. Discuss whether you think they earned the right to be in the club.

8. The kids had the opportunity to swim with Oliver, the whale shark. Is that something you would like to do? Why or why not?

9. Would you like to visit Chichen Itza? If so, what would you most like to see during your visit?

# Built-In Book Club

# Bring It to Life!

1. The Maya had many legends. For example, in the mystery, the legend of Kukulkan as a young boy explained why earthquakes happen in July. Make up your own Maya legend and share it with the class.

2. At the Chichen Itza ruins, the kids learn about the Maya ball games. Izzy tells the kids that there is no written record of the rules for the game. Using what you learned in the mystery and your own ideas, write the rules of the game. Be creative!

3. Design a new book cover for The Mystery at the Maya Ruins. You can draw the cover design yourself, or use computer software to

*Book Club*

create it.  Be sure to make up your own icons to run down the right side of the cover.

4. In the mystery, Grant teaches Christina what he learned about the Maya numbering system. Now, it's your turn to write them.  Remember, the shell is 0, the dot is 1, and the bar is 5. Use the following rules to write numbers.  Can your partner guess your numbers?  Remember to keep a space between the first, second, and third positions when writing numbers larger than 19.

| | | | Examples | | | |
|---|---|---|---|---|---|---|
| 3rd Position | For numbers > 399 | shell = 0 x 20 x 20<br>dot = 1 x 20 x 20<br>line = 5 x 20 x 20 | | | | ▬ |
| 2nd Position | For numbers 20-399 | shell = 0 x 20<br>dot = 1 x 20<br>line = 5 x 20 | | ●●● | ●● ▬ | ⬭ |
| 1st Position | For numbers 0-19 | shell = 0 x 1<br>dot = 1 x 1<br>line = 5 x 1 | ●●●● ▬▬▬ | ⬭ | ▬ | ●●●● ▬▬ |
| | | | 19 | 60<br>+ 0<br>―――<br>60 | 240<br>+ 10<br>―――<br>250 | 2000<br>0<br>+ 14<br>―――<br>2014 |

# MAYA Trivia

1. The four main structures in a Maya temple complex are a pyramid, an observatory, sacrificial altars, and a ball court.

2. The Maya used brushes made with animal hair and quills as writing tools.

3. The Maya calendar included 18 months of 20 days each, plus 1 month of 5 days.

4. Balls used in Maya ballgames were made of rubber and weighed about 8 pounds. They could cause severe injury to players!

5. The Maya loved jewelry, especially items of jade and gold. Jade was one of the most common items traded by the Maya.

6. Maya temples were decorated with brightly colored carvings of jaguars, snakes, birds, and turtles.

7. The Maya numbering system is based on the numbers 0 through 20.

8. Maya children were named according to the day they were born. Every day had a specific name assigned to it for both boys and girls.

9. A Maya myth: the Maya priests could create goblins called *aluxob*. These goblins would help the farmer grow corn by protecting his field and summoning the rain gods—but only if the goblin was well cared for.

10. Maya medicine men used advanced techniques. They sewed up wounds with human hair, healed fractures, made fake teeth using jade and turquoise, and used iron to fill cavities.

# Glossary

**alma mater:** the university a person attended

**SAD chasm:** a large hole, like a crater

**SAD contortion:** the act of twisting or deforming the shape of something

**distinctive:** unique or different from others

**foretell:** predict

**SAD meander:** move or roam around

**mythological:** related to legends and folklore

*Glossary*

**profusely:** abundantly; excessively

**spectacle:** a scene

**starboard:** the right side of a boat or plane

**stifling:** very hot, making it hard to breathe

**tenacious:** determined to complete a task

**translucent:** not completely clear or transparent, but clear enough to allow light to pass through

# Visit the <u>carolemarshmysteries.com</u> website to:

- Join the Carole Marsh Mysteries™ Fan Club!

- Write a letter to Christina, Grant, Mimi, or Papa!

- Cast your vote for where the next mystery should take place!

- Find fascinating facts about the countries where the mysteries take place!

- Track your reading on an international map!

- Take the Fact or Fiction online quiz!

- Find out where the Mystery Girl is flying next!